PREY TARGETS

PREY TARGETS

JOSHUA HORVATH

Ordering Information:

For orders and inquiries, please contact:
1-888-404-1388
www.goldtouchpress.com
book.orders@goldtouchpress.com

Printed in the United States of America

The year is 2515, and Earth is slowly healing after humankind nearly destroyed it. Humankind now lives among the stars in far off galaxies, but once again humankind is facing overpopulation and limited resources. So thousands of robotic probes were sent out to nearby galaxies to explore their moons and planets, for possible new natural resources and possible colonization. Several candidates were found but one stuck out the most to the United States colony. A huge bluish green planet about the size of Neptune has been found. The probes found that the planet is carpeted in plant and tree like organisms. The oxygen levels are very high making only two major problems to deal with super storms which are powered by the oxygen levels, plus the high levels make the air poisonous to humans, but the dangers were well worth the abundance of natural resources.

So a research team was assembled to explore the planet which has been named Aisha which means life and hope, but they will be escorted by a special security force, for images of the local wildlife looks to be very dangerous. Leading the security force was Mike Maze or aka sweet candy, and my name is Charlie an artificial intelligent robotic drone. I have been redesigned just for Aisha. I am now shaped like a jet with two sets of bat wings giving me the ability to glide over Aisha like most wildlife. I have also been fitted with new arms to help Mike with anything he might need, for it's my job to keep an eye on Mike and keep in touch with our space station Morgan that will be hovering above Aisha, by updating her with each part of the mission so if anything goes wrong Mike can be helped out, for Morgan is an advanced robotic space station that is self-aware with artificial intelligences to back her up as well. I, Mike, and the richer team were now in a free fall on Aisha through its thick dense algae bloomed filled atmosphere. Good thing is due to the less amount of gravity on Aisha everything falls slower than it does on Earth, but falling slow also means attracting some unwanted attention by some of the local wildlife. It was hard to see due to Aisha is always in twilight like state, for Aisha is just out of reach of its twin stars to get light like we did on Earth. Aisha light is like going outside really early in the morning on Earth with the sun just coming up. It's real faded and not that bright only parts of the sky are lit up.

Now only inches in front of us were a small group of massive creatures that looked like stick bugs mixed with flying squirrels. They have long paddle-like legs something like you would find on a whale, connected to those paddle like legs is a thin membrane like skin. The creatures were very cool but bizarre looking, for they are light brown in color with dark black polka dots covering their bodies. They also had five big round eyes two on each side of their heads and one big one just above their mouth. Lastly they also have a massive wing structure that looks like old leaves that have been lying around the backyard all winter long. Then something seemed to spook the creatures away, for they seemed to be trying to get away fast. That's when we got our first sight of one of Aisha predators, a huge two armed elongated tail creature that was dark green in color. It had several eyes at least twenty of them and it had strange looking worm-like appendages coming off its fingers three on each hand. It finally approached a few of our researchers and it's chest opened up and out came tentacle-like appendages that wrapped around the researchers which must have a substance on them that must paralyze their prey, for the researchers couldn't even scream. It then stuffed them into its elongated mouth and blood ran down its chest. Mike finally got a hold of his gun, for the winds are really strong. Mike got a shot off and hit the hot air balloon like appendage on the creatures back, and it exploded violently, must of have been filled with some type of gas like methane.

Once we were safely on the planet's surface the first thing on our to do list was setting up base camp but that was a hard thing to do around here, for tree like organisms cover the planet's surface, but once we got walking around with snow crunching under our feet the shorter trees must of got spooked, for they actually started running away making room for our base. Then we heard a loud bellowing like sound coming right at us, it was a stampede of massive big round yellow six legged creatures. They had root like appendages covering their bodies with two elongated mouthparts that looked like two elephant trunks that were glued together. Then right behind them was a pack of massive ghostly white translucent creatures with six long powerful legs, and two rows of needle shaped teeth, and no visible ears. The big yellow creatures crushed everything in their paths including much of our equipment, and a few researchers. Then one of the yellow creatures ran over an icy spot making it smack up against a tree, and bleed out. The rest of us tried to flee behind a tree, but the massive predators found us more interesting as a meal and used us like chew toys. Mike opened fire injuring one of the creatures then finally the military bots were dropped in. They used their laser cannons to chop through some of the creatures like butter while other bots let loose their grenade launchers on the creatures, and the loud sounds from the grenades scared them away. It also scared away several of the small trees. They took off in a dead run for the thicker parts of the forest.

These little trees stood up on four massive roots like stilts that they also seem to use to walk or run around. The little trees then went straight up like trees do on Earth, and they seemed to be covered in a bark like covering like red woods back on Earth, and just like the massive trees surrounding them the smaller trees had cotton candy like structures growing on top on them, for just below the cotton candy like structure they had short twisted branches on them. High up in the canopy of the massive trees seemed to be a whole another world of creatures, and another weird thing was that all of the massive trees were connected like one big network by vines looking tudes that glowed a bright blue color. It was now time to gather our thoughts, and samples. So the military bots went with the researchers to explore life on the forest floor and me and Mike were going to explore the canopy.

Once we got to the canopy everything seemed to go quiet, but we were fooled I detected life just couldn't see it when all of a sudden the trees came to life, for there was several leaf like structures covering the trees that were actually creatures, for their bodies were a dark translucent blue you could see straight through the creatures you could see their organs and everything plus their bodies were shaped just like leafs. They also had a long dinosaur like tail with a leaf looking appendage on the end of it. They also had six long legs with hockey stick looking appendages covering their backs. Another weird thing about these creatures was their elongated fingers that they had on their front two hands. Last they had four big round eyes two on each side of their heads. The creatures approached us slowly, not really sure what to make of us. Suddenly the creatures started acting weird like they were scared of something.

The creatures then picked us up like we were toys, for they were five times our size. They took us up inside the cotton candy like structures on the top of the trees. We didn't know what to think. We then peeped through the leafs and seen several shadow-like figures jump over us. We then heard screaming and gunshots. These strange blue creatures were actually protecting us. We jumped out of the cotton candy structure and on the ground the robots and researchers were getting ripped to pieces by a massive whiptail scorpion looking creatures. The creature was actual dislocating its jaws like a snake, and swallowing the researchers' whole. You could see the imprints of their screaming faces inside the creature's bellies. Mike and the robots opened fired on the creatures but their bullets and lasers seem to bounce right off the creatures' tough exoskeleton. One the creatures swallowed a robot whole, and the Robot processed its self-destruct operation and the robot exploded killing the creature from the inside, pieces of it went flying in all directions. One robot opened up its flamethrowers killing two of the creatures torching them to death. The Robots then went on a bug killing spree burning as many of the creatures as they could but the creatures were extremely fast and agile.

Then the wind started to pick up, and the skies got totally pitch black Morgan sent me a message of a huge super storm that was heading in our direction. The Whiptail scorpion like creatures sniffed the air, and headed for cover. We then headed for cover but it was so hard to see and breathe, for the wind speeds were well over four hundred mph and getting stronger with each passing moment. The Robots followed when we found a notch in a tree and stuffed ourselves in it, but it was too late for the Robots, for several lighting balls came along with the super storms. Lighting balls are huge balls of electricity that hover a few inches off the ground and if they are triggered by any type of movement they release thousands of volts of electricity in several different directions. A few Robots trigger the balls frying all of them in the process. The storm then dropped hailstones the size of basketballs and raindrops the size of softballs down upon us. Thousands of twisters passed over us with wind speeds reaching over a thousand miles per hour. Things on this planet must be built for storms, for the tree shook a little but no real damage at all. The storm finally cleared twelve hours later. Once we got out of the notch there were alien creatures everywhere feeding on all the fruit or vegetables like things lying on the forest floor. We then saw those bluish creatures that saved us and we then got a better look at them.

They had no noses, they seem to breathe through their skin, and the way they feed was really neat they don't have a mouth, so they actually produce some type of digestive chemical that comes from their elongated fingers, it turns their food into a liquid form, and then they use their elongated fingers to drink the liquid like a milkshake. Morgan then sent us new directions to where our new supplies are, and equipment that could be picked up. Just feet in front us we came across several more creatures that were feeding. The first one looks like a big green bubble that seemed to be floating along with a bluish glow inside of it. The creature was now feeding on a fruit that looked like a cross between a squash and a gored. The creature had a huge flower shaped mouth part that swallowed the fruit whole. Once it reached the body you could see the fruit dissolve in moments it was cool. The next set of creatures we came up on were dark purple, and round with skin that looked like netting. On the front of their bodies were light blue heads also with netting like skin. They also had another light blue ball on the inside of their heads with three white ball-like appendages on them. The creatures also seemed to be floating a few feet off the ground. They seemed to be feeding on a huge fruit that looked like a huge green strawberry with strange looking holes in it.

They had mouthparts like a butterfly, and seemed to be sucking the juices out of the fruit. When they were done feeding on the fruits they looked like old raisins that had been sitting out in the sun for a while. The forest then seemed to get quiet when we then heard strange noises. Mike then noticed we were surrounded by a small group of those ghostly white predators from earlier. Mike drew his gun and opened fire. I started shooting flares in all directions. My flares scared a few of the creatures away. Mike then shot and killed one of the creatures, but another bigger one kept coming at him. He then drew a machete from the side of his suit stabbing the creature in the face until one of the creature's eyeballs fell to the forest floor. The creature came at Mike again. Mike then stabbed it in the head but not just before it almost ripped his arm off. Mike was hurt badly and I was unable to contact Morgan. So I picked up Mike and flew him to a gap between some trees Mike was bleeding badly, but if he didn't get help soon he would surely die. The creature had disappeared. Then out of know where came those bluish creatures from earlier that helped us out, but this time they were in a group of five and they approached Mike, and one of creatures laid it's hand on Mike's arm and just stared at it for a few moments. The creature then picked Mike up and laid him on his back. It looked back at me as it started to walk away like it wanted me to follow it. So I followed, and we came to another gap in the forest where the creature broke some branches off a tree, and laid Mike on them. Then all of the creatures disappeared into the canopy where I saw several different light patterns going on.

A little while passed and the blue creatures came back down from the trees but they were not alone. Three new massive creatures came down with them they also had elongated bodies, legs, fingers, and toes which are wide. These new creatures also had long dinosaur like tails, and appendages on their backs. The difference between the blue creatures is their appendages these creatures' appendages looked like spines that are a dark purple in color. Their skin is a dark purplish black with dark blue stripes covering their bodies. Also unlike the blue creature's only part of their bodies are translucent. Only their sides and their bellies are. Like the blue creatures they have two big round eyes two on each side of their heads. They also have long necks and elongated faces that are axe shaped, and mouthparts that are elongated but look like tentacles you find on a squid. Last they have a small frill that extends from their foreheads. Last they have small spines that extend off from the top of their legs. Their back legs looks are actually shaped like legs you find on a cricket. These new creatures then disappeared into the woods for a little while then came back with a strange looking purple plant. The creature then pulled some leaves off a nearby tree and handed it off to one of the blue creatures. The blue creature then used the substance that comes out of their fingers to turn the plant into a liquid. The blue creature then wrapped the leaves and the liquid plant around Mike's arm. They sat with us for a few hours until they disappeared into the canopy. Mike then came around and started walking around real slow and that same time Morgan finally got in touch with us, but for some reason her computers went offline for a while.

There was bad news that all our supplies we were heading for had been stolen by another team, but these guys are all gun happy shooting first, and asking questions later. So Morgan was dropping off supplies in another area that actually wasn't too far away, but we would have to cut through some swamp land and a nesting ground for another one of Aisha predators. Then out of know where came these trigger happy idiots with one screaming "this stuff must be yours". They were driving massive trucks made to go all terrain. They were from the African and Russian colonies. These guys are usually pretty cool, but these guys were just here to make some fast money, and we were just in their way. They then drew their weapons on us saying we will take you as prisoners. You might be worth something. Mike was still too weak to fight back, but once again our blue friends came to our aid, and with one swipe of the creature's finger it decapitated four men. Then out of the canopy came those other creatures that helped Mike earlier, the ones with the frill. They were smashing the front ends of the trucks. The poachers then opened fire on the creatures. Then one poacher got scared and started running away when he tripped head first on a huge super-sized steel trap they had planted splattering his brains all over the forest floor. Then the creatures just started stepping on the poachers smashing them into the ground like bugs, so once all the poachers were all dead the creatures once again disappeared into the canopy. The good thing was our supplies were now right in front of us including two big containers of advanced military robots. Mike was now back to normal, but knew that we had no hope of collecting much data on Aisha. So he made me contact Morgan. She was now sending several probes down to collect as much info on the planet as possible. Another problem we were facing was winter that was fast approaching, for the planet goes even farther from its twin stars and when that happens the planet goes totally pitch black for about three months and the temps dropped to negative sixty and below and the super storms continue mostly massive winds and sleet the size of basketballs. So it was time to get off this rock, but the only way to do that was go on a three day hike to the mountains on the Eastern side of the planet, so we gathered our supplies and prepared the Robots for our hike.

A few miles into the hike we came to a shallow river that was covered in strange looking brown rocks that seemed to be moving, and seemed to have gray looking root like appendages that went all the way around them. We just kept going then we noticed some creatures swimming around in the water small fish sized translucent creatures that had light brown insides, and a long slender translucent tail. There were schools of them everywhere. We also noticed a light grey watermelon shaped creature that looked like a prehistoric fish with human looking teeth, but we just continued with our hike. Then we came across a tree bigger than any tree we seen so far.The vines on the tree seemed to be alive when a strange acid like liquid seemed to be some type of digestive juices was being shot at us from a tentacle like appendage. We then got a look at the creatures and decided to call them tree jellies, for that is what they looked like giant jellyfish. We then ran like heck and came to a huge waterfall that was feeding a lake that looked like it was created by massive impact by an asteroid or comet. Along the banks were bunches of creatures that looked like a cross between a starfish and a spider. The creature had a starfish like body, legs and all and in between the starfish looking legs it had spider looking eyes, it also had a big spider like butt on one end of its body. The creature also had four eyes, two in the front and two on the very back of its head. The creatures seemed to be very friendly. Then came a small group burrowing like creatures light blue and translucent with eight legs four on each side of their bodies. Then the ground started to shake and we heard loud booming noises like thunder. We also got a sight of how the tree jellies reproduce by injecting their eggs into live prey. Their babies hatch eating their prey from the inside out. Then out of nowhere came three huge herds of creatures, two very massive, and one species a little smaller, a two legged winged creature that was very colorful. The creature looked like it once was four legged but over time it's legs fused together. The second creature was massive with light purple skin and a short little tail. This creature also had a dark red axe like appendage of their heads with dark red air sack like appendage on their throats like a bullfrog.

This four eyed creature was the only creature we saw so far with hoofed feet. The last creatures we seen were the biggest creatures we have seen on Aisha so far, bigger than any dinosaur ever found on Earth they had big wide padded feet like you would find on an Elephant, but the strangest thing about the creatures were the bat arm looking appendage they had on the top of their heads. It also had a long dinosaur-like tail with several long colorful hairs covering their bellies. Then all of a sudden the creatures started going crazy something was coming up behind them. A titanic sized predator that looked like a spider crab, but with twelve legs and elongated claws. The creature is also a translucent gray with spine like appendages covering its body. It was now chasing the herding creatures. When all of a sudden the creatures started coming right at us. The first creature just jumped or glided right over us but the next two herds of creatures almost trampled us so we hid in a nearby log. A few of the Robots opened fire on the creatures but it had no effect, and the Robots were crushed into the ground like a soda can that got run over by a car. Not wanting to take any chances we decided to go around the lake sticking with the dry land because it's a little safer. So we finally made it around the lake when we came up on a flooded forest that was partly frozen over and in the distance was those ghostly white predator creatures from a few days ago, and they were working alongside a new translucent predator creature that was a little smaller than them, but these new creatures looked like they were aquatic as well, for the fins on their back, and sides plus they had a long fish like tail. Both creatures seem to be preparing for the winter, for they were stripping flesh off a huge creature we've haven't seen alive yet, and putting the flesh into clear cocoon like things and taking them up into the canopy or down into their muddy burrows. We soon realized we were surrounded by both types of creatures there was nowhere to hide we had to fight. The Robots opened fire and Mike locked and loaded and when a creature got close enough he fired trying to save on bullets for there was hundreds of the smaller creatures. The creatures seem to be overwhelming us for everyone shot three more seemed to pop up. The Robots were being ripped to pieces all around us. Mike was taken down by the same creatures, and stuffed into a cocoon. I had no idea what to do. I flew out of reach of the creatures, and I contacted Morgan she was already had a plan she was sending in Kristin Mike's ex-wife long crazy story there, but Kristen is actually a cyborg, for she was severely hurt in battle and had to be put back together she is now more machine than human but a great warrior at that. Morgan sent Kristin and about two hundred new advanced battlebots to get Mike. The problem was there was no safe place to drop her other than the mountain Mike, and I were heading for, or back where we first got dropped off. Morgan decided to drop Kristin and the Robots off at the mountains, but that was really far away, but Morgan had no choice. Morgan then decided to deploy some military drones to buy Mike some time. The drones flew in firing at the creatures from all directions; this gave Mike time to cut his way out of the cocoon but he was still trapped in the burrow. Mike soon realized he still had a sun boom. It is a boom that lets off a blast as bright as the Earth's sun on a warm summer's day. Bang Bang the boom went off blinding the creatures, for their eyes weren't used to such bright lights.

Mike got out of the burrow and ran like heck into the woods with me right behind him. He kept running and running until we came to another waterfall. Mike jumped off the waterfall down into the river. It was a good thing that the river was peaceful. He swam over to the shore where he just laid on the cold snow cover ground. Mike was now cold for the water was freezing, and the air itself was already cold. Mike knew he had to warm up or he would catch hypothermia so we gathered the driest plant matter we could find Mike and I then set a flare to it giving him a nice warm fire to keep warm at the same time the snow started picking up a little. So Mike and I found a small hollowed out log, and some more plant matter, and he fell fast asleep, and I kept an eye out for any danger. Eight hours have passed Mike was now awake and reenergized problem was we had no idea where we were so we contacted Morgan we found out two things we still had a whole day's hike to reach the mountains, and Kristin had been attacked, and she had been caught by those scorpion like creatures that we ran into before. Strange thing was her Robots were missing and they went off radar. We decided to find Kristin, but once again we had no supplies, and only a knife for a weapon.

Morgan was now sending in a minnie probe to check in on Kristen so far so good she was actually using a laser knife to cut her way out of the scorpions food cocoons. Those cocoons were very thick and slimy, but she finally made it out, and surrounding her were parts of the robots The creatures were actually building nest out of their body parts. We finally made it to the massive tree where she was being kept. Mike had me fly him up to the nearest opening in the tree where he jumped down into the tree and just moments later he had Kristin in his arms. He then threw her up and over his head trying to protect her from the scorpion like creatures. Mike then got back into the hole in the tree screaming "Charlie take her to a safe place! I'll hold these guys off", for he was using his body as a wall to keep them in the tree. Mike then went back down into the tree as I flew away with Kristin moments later the massive tree exploded into thousands of pieces. It was raining tree and creature parts. Mike had sacrificed himself to save us. I could hear Kristin crying as I laid her down on the soft moss like plants. About an hour later Kristin was ready to go, for winter was fast approaching even faster than Morgan calculated every hour seemed to be getting colder. So we continued on our journey to the mountains all Kristin kept talking about was taking a warm shower and going shopping must be a human girl thing.

A few hours passed and it was really quiet until a group of shadowy figures kept darting through the woods they seemed to be following us. We were then surrounded by a pack of canine like creatures the size of school buses. That had strange looking appendages on their heads and throats with two rows of razor sharp and wide paws and big round eyes two on each side of their heads. They seemed to growling at us these creatures seemed to be the wolves of this planet. The creatures were getting closer and closer then all of sudden something seemed to spook them, for they ran straight for the woods as fast as they could. Except for one of them the creature was biting at Kristen's legs she then reached for a broken stick only inches in front of her, and started stabbing the creature in the head over and over until it retreated into a different set of woods. We then seen a swarm of massive sized bizarre bug looking creatures fly over with each fly over they seemed to be getting lower and lower. Kristin then started to roll around on the ground then she laid completely still the creatures seemed to give up interest and kept flying over. Then in the distance a group of creatures that looked like a cross between Jaguar and a

Mink were keeping their eyes on us, but they vanished into the forest. Kristin then asked me to help her find anything that I could to make some type of weapons for that was too many close calls with no protection. We gathered several branches and Kristin used her knife to make a few spheres, but that is better than nothing. We then continued our hike when we came upon three huge trucks that looked like the ones that the trigger happy poachers from earlier had, but these trucks were covered in blood and it was fresh. Afraid of what could be lurking around we searched the trucks as fast as we could. We found several supplies and new weapons that could be of use. We then headed out, we were then contacted by Morgan a massive snow storm was heading straight for us. Kristin decided to backtrack because of the trucks we found earlier was a tanker truck and we could do that as shelter. Once inside the tanker Kristin blasted a small hole in the top to let out the smoke and I was gathering plant material to burn for Kristin was going to one of my flares to make a fire to keep us from freezing. Three hours passed and finally the snow gave up a little but it was cold as heck outside, But we had to continue with our hike Morgan informed us that the temps are now in the negative digits and the only wildlife that's out and about are hungry predators so we have to be extra careful.

We had been walking for about an hour when we started hearing strange clicking noises coming from a small group of those walking trees. There were sheep sized creatures that were nesting in the trees. It was a trade off the bird like gliding rodents gave the trees an earlier warning system for predators and they gave them a safe warm home. We then approached the trees to check the creatures out they seemed to be very friendly, for they came right out of their nest to check us out. They kept rubbing on Kristin when we heard something heading for us. The bird-like creatures started to click like crazy coming up on us as a huge pack of those wolf-like creatures, the ones in the front of the pack were even bigger than the others we saw earlier. Kristin started firing at them shooting one of them in the leg making it drop and roll. She also shot one in the head blowing off the side of its face. We kept running when we came to a thick dense forest that was on a steep hill it was really hard for Kristin to make it up when the huge blue creature that helped me and

Mike earlier picked up Kristin and laid her in a nearby tree that was on top of the hill. The creature then started picking up those wolf-like creatures and smashing them on the ground until there was nothing left of them. Another group of the blue creatures were picking up tree branches and using them like baseball bats to slap the wolf like creatures around. Finally the wolf creatures retreated back into another set of the woods. The blue creatures seemed to be checking Kristin out to make sure she was okay. Once they were done looking Kristin over the creatures disappeared into the canopy. By this time the wind was getting really strong with temps dropping even lower we had to get out of this storm. Morgan then contacted us there was a canyon we could cut through to get us to the mountains. About an hour passed and we finally made it to the entrance of the canyon things were different here it was warmer with only traces of snow on the ground. Once inside the canyon walls the temperature was so much warmer, for the ground was covered in steam vents and gushers. There must be an underground volcano nearby. The ground here was solid in some spots other spots felt like we were walking on a waterbed. A light orange plant that resembled grass carpeted the land here we nicknamed it carrot grass.

We then came across herds of two legged bird like creatures must have been thousands of them. These creatures stood on two legs like an ostrich with two wide feet. They also had four arms on their chest with four wide hands. The arms and hands looked like the ones you would see on a raptor dinosaur, but their faces were very bird like, for they looked like robins. They were also covered in feather like fur that is dark blue, black, and red in color. They also had short feather-like appendages on their backs and heads. As we walked around the creatures it didn't seem to bother them, for they were too busy feeding upon the carrot grass. They use those four long arms to feed.

We continued our hike but for some reason the bird creatures kept their distance from the canyon walls. Then out of know where came a new predator, and a new group of advanced military robots, for the military fleet that was going to pick us up sent these robots in to help us with the rest of our hike or journey. Perfect timing for out of know where came translucent tentacles with razor sharp appendages on the end them. One of the tentacles knocked Kristen to her feet then wrapping her up the tentacle acted like a snake crushing its prey until there was no movement suffocating it to death. Also like a snake the tentacle would dislocate and could open up twice its size to swallow its prey whole. The more Kristin moved the more the tentacle squeezed the robots finally came to her aid using their laser cannons to splice their tentacles in half. The robots then opened fire with their armor piercing rounds killing the boomerang shaped creatures. The creatures seemed to use tether like appendages to hold themselves on to the canyon's walls. Then the predators flew right over us like a glider, for the creatures had a flap of skin that would lift up and help them catch the wind currents to glide away.

Kristin was barely able to move, for the creature's tentacles had crushed some of her internal organs. So I picked her up when we came to a natural spiral staircase of rock, water, and plant matter that seemed too interconnected to make something like a natural bridge into the mountains. I started to fly Kristin up the bridge when out of nowhere a group of creatures knocked me right out the air. I rebooted several hours later with pieces of military bots scattered all around me, and it was even colder and darker than before and Kristin knew where to be found. Moments passed and I was able to repair myself. I then went airborne to try and find Kristin. I finally picked up on her pheromones or smell. All living creatures give off some type of smell. Kristin was now being held prisoner at a huge poaching base this was the main setup, for those trigger happy idiots from earlier, and these guys were heavily armed. I tried to contact Morgan but she seemed to be unreachable. Then a light bulb went off like I said before all things give off a smell even big scary alien predators.

Well as you know we have been collecting samples through our whole trip even me and the one that smelled the worst came from those scorpion like creatures so in the shadows I sprayed down the poachers camp, and hid in the shadows waiting for the action to begin. About an hour passed when it sounded like a herd of elephants was coming in, but instead of elephants it was thousands of scorpion creatures and they were ticked, for they don't like to be woken up in the cold, but they always can go for a late night snack. They stormed the camp butchering almost everyone. I then swooped in getting Kristin the heck out of there as quick as I could. But with everything that was going on I got lost, I was now entering a huge forest covered in volcanic ash and acid snow. But I was now on a time clock, for Kristin was dying. I then came to a clearing where my sensors started picking up some type of life form one of those poachers had followed us he started firing at us I dropped Kristin in the process. The poacher had a gun right to Kristen's head about ready to pull the trigger when the bushes behind him started to shake and a large group of those ghostly white translucent creatures me and Mike ran into earlier came out, one of them took its claws in the poachers mouth then tearing off the top of the poachers head devouring his brain. I then headed for Kristin but it was too late she had already vanished, for she had rolled into a nearby gysher made water hole where eel cookie cutter shark like creatures were trying to tear the flesh from Kristen's body. The ghostly looking translucent creatures then headed for me when I had an all systems shutdown total loss of power.

I awoke some time later, and I was aboard Morgan with Becca, a robotics expert saying good job Charlie you've done well, for everyone that goes to Aisha are just Prey Targets for that world. Then right beside me was Kristin in a healing chamber with everyone hoping for the best, and I was already getting loaded with details with one of Aisha moons me and Kristin's next mission to see you there.

www.ingramcontent.com/pod-product-compliance
Lightning Source LLC
Chambersburg PA
CBHW022043050726
47591CB00003B/926